Chicken Licken

Jackie Walter and Andy Rowland

W
FRANKLIN WATTS
LONDON•SYDNEY

One day, a silly young chick called Chicken Licken was scratching around for some corn. Suddenly, an acorn fell from the sky and landed on her head with a bump.

"Oh no!" she yelped dizzily.
"The sky is falling in. I must go
and tell the king the terrible
news! I must tell everyone!"

She hurried off in a panic. Soon she met her friend Henny Penny.

"Where are you going in such a rush?" asked Henny Penny.

"The sky is falling in!" cried young Chicken Licken. "Some fell on my head and it really hurt. I'm going to tell the king the terrible news!"

Henny Penny was worried. "I will come with you to see the king," she clucked.

At the duck pond, they met their friend Ducky Lucky.

"Where are you two going in such a rush?" asked Ducky Lucky.

"The sky is falling in!"
cried Henny Penny.
"It fell on my head!" babbled
Chicken Licken. "We're going
to tell the king the
terrible news!"

"This is awful news! I will come with you to see the king," quacked Ducky Lucky.

Down the lane, they met their friend Goosey Loosey.

"Where are you three going in such a rush?" asked Goosey Loosey.

"The sky is falling in!"
quacked Ducky Lucky.
"It fell on my head!" cried
Chicken Licken. "We're going
to tell the king the terrible news!"

"This is dreadful. I will come with you to see the king," honked Goosey Loosey in a panic.

By the hedge, they met Foxy Loxy.
Foxy Loxy was feeling a bit peckish after
a nice morning relaxing by his den.

"Where are you four delicious-looking birds going in such a rush?" asked Foxy Loxy.

"The sky is falling in!" cried Chicken Licken.

"It fell on her head!" clucked Henny Penny.

"We're off to tell the king!" quacked Ducky Lucky.

"We're all doomed!" honked Goosey Loosey.

"I see!" said the cunning old fox with a grin. "May I ask, do you know the way to the king's palace?"

The four silly birds all looked at each other. "No!" they said. "We didn't think about which way to go!"

"Let me help. I can show you exactly how to get there. Just follow me. Through this little door is the quickest way," smiled Foxy Loxy, licking his lips.

The four silly birds didn't stop to think for even one minute. They followed Foxy Loxy straight into his den in the hedge. The king never did hear about the sky falling in and Foxy Loxy wasn't hungry for ages!

About the story

Chicken Licken is a folk tale. Some people trace it back to Buddhist scriptures from 2,500 years ago. It was part of an oral tradition, and first published in English in 1840. It is especially popular in America, where it is also known as *Chicken Little*. One moral that can be taken from the story is the importance of not believing everything one is told. However, in some versions, Chicken Licken escapes and does warn the king. Then the moral of the story can be having courage.

Be in the story!

Imagine you are Chicken Licken. How do you feel when the other animals start worrying too?

Now imagine you are Foxy Loxy. How do you feel when the birds walk right up to your den and then inside it?

Franklin Watts
First published in Great Britain in 2015 by The Watts Publishing Group

Series Editor: Jackie Hamley
Series Advisor: Catherine Glavina
Series Designer: Cathryn Gilbert

A CIP catalogue record for this book is available
from the British Library.

The artwork for this story first appeared in
Leapfrog Fairy Tales: Chicken Licken

ISBN 978 1 4451 4444 3 (hbk)
ISBN 978 1 4451 4446 7 (pbk)
ISBN 978 1 4451 4445 0 (library ebook)
ISBN 978 1 4451 4447 4 (ebook)

Printed in China

Franklin Watts
An imprint of
Hachette Children's Group
Part of The Watts Publishing Group
Carmelite House
50 Victoria Embankment
London EC4Y 0DZ

An Hachette UK Company
www.hachette.co.uk

www.franklinwatts.co.uk

FSC
www.fsc.org
MIX
Paper from
responsible sources
FSC® C104740